THE CHRISTMAS STRANGER

THE CHRISTMAS STRANGER

LISA MARIE NICOLE

Hope and Glory Press LLC

The Christmas Stranger

Nicole Cimino stood on her front porch as she watched the men from the bank take away the furniture from her house that they had just repossessed.

"You have no heart!" She yelled at them, "It's two weeks before Christmas!" The men paid her no mind as they went about their work. When the last piece of furniture was loaded, the one man approached her and handed her a card. "What's this?" She asked. He said, "It's the bank's phone number if you want to reclaim your furniture, but you have to pay the balance." Nicole looked at him with tears in her eyes and said, "With what?" "My husband died in a car accident and left us 60,000 in debt." I have been trying to pay that off for a year now. " I can't work, and I have a handicapped child that I am trying to care for! So you can keep your furniture! we'll sleep on the floor!" She threw the card at him and went back into the empty house.

A tiny voice brought her back to reality, "Mommy, are you ok" It was her daughter Samantha. Friends called her Sammy for short. Nicole turned around and saw her 10-year-old leaning on crutches with a look of sadness on her face. She had been born with brittle bone disease. It is a disability that makes your bones fragile. She has 26 screws in her little body from all the broken bones that she sustained over the years. She cannot walk without crutches for fear of falling again. The doctors said she should live a long life, providing that she gets the lifesaving surgery that she needs. The surgery costs around 100 thousand dollars, and between her medication and the surgery, Nicole just doesn't have the money.

Since her husband had a good job, she didn't need to work, so she dedicated her life to taking care of her daughter and homeschooling her. She does not have insurance, so she goes on everyday praying for a miracle. She does everything to make sure her little girl's precious time on this earth is joyful and fulfilling as can be. She prays to God every day for a sign.

Sammy walked up to her mom and handed her a tiny box, "What's this honey?" she asked her fragile daughter "It's from my piggy bank, it's for you to buy us a new bed." Nicole, with tears in her eyes, opened the box and saw five twenty-dollar bills in it. "Oh Sammy you keep your money, it's yours". "No!" she shouted, "It's ours. Daddy gave it to me. I have Been saving it. He said only to use it in an emergency, so I am giving it to you." Nicole started to cry as she hugged her daughter gently, then they sat in the empty house on their sleeping bags in front of the big window and watched the snow start to fall outside.

Nicole was awakened during the night in need of the bathroom. Climbing over her sleeping bag, trying not to wake Sammy, she walked to the bathroom. Thank God they left the toilet paper, she thought to herself. She planned on calling the church food pantry to deliver food and ask them to drop off some furniture from the local thrift shop. One thing she had going for her was that she used to volunteer at St. John's church office that was in the town next door to where she lived, and she knew lots of people in town that helped her when she needed anything. Now is that time. As she was going back to bed, she heard a loud bang outside. It sounded like a car accident, but who would be driving down here in the middle of the night? She looked at the clock and it was 1 am, She lived in a very deserted area. She ran to the front door and threw it open, she was taken back by the amount of snow that has accumulated during the night, There in the street she saw two cars, one was flipped over and was on fire and the other was embedded in a nearby oak tree. Since she lived in a very secluded area of Pennsylvania and the snow was knee-deep, she knew that she was their only chance of survival.

Running into the darkness with nothing but a bathrobe and slippers, she slipped on the icy new fallen snow and got back up and kept going, her feet were freezing and wet, but it didn't stop her, she kept on running towards the car in the tree, because she saw that the other one was completely engulfed in flames now and that person's chance of survival was very slim, she made the sign of the cross and prayed for his soul as she walked past that car. The heat from the flames warmed her up a little, but she kept thinking of the person in that car. when she got closer to the car in the tree, she noticed that there was a person slumped over the steering wheel, it was a man, by his white hair she guessed he was an older gentleman, he was unconscious and blood was oozing from his head, she noticed the driver side door was open from impact, so she reached in and pulled the man to safety, she was strong for 120 lbs., I guess all the years of carrying Sam back and forth to the bathroom made her stronger. She pulled the man all the way to her front door, and then she heard the car burst into flames, then she passed out from the cold.

Nicole heard her husband calling her, "Nikki wake up, Sam needs you". She opened her eyes and all she saw was white above her she could not feel her hands or feet, but she was alive.

She looked around and saw a small patch of ground nearby and the man was lying there, My God! she thought to herself, is he dead? With all of her might she picked herself up and dragged her freezing body over to the man, she felt for a pulse and he was still alive, how? She had no idea, but she knew she had to act fast. She whispered to the man, 'Hello? Can you hear me? coughing violently, he said "yes." Don't talk. She said to him, "I'm here to help you." He pulled her arm down so that her face was next to his and said, "Thank you" My name is Joseph.

She looked into his eyes and saw that he was in bad shape, if he didn't get help soon, he might not make it. He was burned badly, and it looked like he had a broken arm as well. She said, "I'll be right back. She went into the house to check on Sammy, but she was still sleeping through it all. Grabbing the phone off the wall, she wasn't surprised to hear silence at the other end; Damn! she yelled; they turned off the phone too! God, she yelled what do I do? " She ran back outside and asked Joseph if he could get up, He said, "I don't know, let me try "She noticed that the snow was getting deeper and deeper, and that the news said that this will be the storm of the century.

Carefully she led the man up the ramp that her husband had built for Sammy, she led him into the empty living room and sat him down on one of the 2 folding chairs she had left, thank God she still had heat for now, until they turned that off as well.

Nicole had her personal belongings in her bathroom, so she went and got some alcohol to clean up the man's cuts and a washcloth and some water to wash his burnt skin down with as she was cleaning him. She heard Sammy scream, "Who is that mommy? Nicole turned around to see the frightened look on her face. It's ok, Sam, this is Joseph, he was in an accident right outside of our house. Joseph looked at her and said, "Hi Sam, May I call you that?" She snapped back," only my friends call me that." "Sam!" Nicole yelled at her daughter, "be nice to him, he was just in an accident," "its ok, Joseph said, "Maybe we can become friends, it looks like we are not going anywhere anytime soon.""Do you have a teapot?" Joseph asked with a smile, "yes, I do, one of the things I still have, Nicole answered." "Great, then a cup of tea sounds great, and thank you for saving my life."" I do not think anything is broken, maybe fractured, but I will live, thanks to you."

As Nicole walked into her kitchen she couldn't help but notice that Joseph looked a lot younger than she first thought, Maybe 60 or so, since she was only 35 that made him older than her. As she was walking back to the living room, she stopped in shock and saw her 10 year old daughter standing next to the man without her crutches, she was wiping down his head with a rag, "Sammy? She yelled, you should not be without your crutches," "It's ok, mom, " she said in a soft voice, I'm leaning against the chair," then she went back to cleaning the man's bloody head. She realized at that moment what she knew for years, that Samatha was a blessing from God to her and the world, look at the way she naturally wants to help people. With a smile on her face, she went over and helped her daughter try to nurse the man back to health.

Nicole was surprised that Sam had warmed up to Joseph so quickly when, just minutes before, she didn't want to say hello to him. She ran to get some wound cream and she and her daughter softly rubbed it on Joseph's burnt head as he winced in pain. Eventually, Sam fell back to sleep. Nicole looked out the window and saw that they were completely snowed in, and it was still coming down. It was now 4am and there was still not a sign of emergency vehicles anywhere the two cars that were in the accident were completely buried in the new fallen snow, leaving no evidence that there was even an accident. She turned around and sighed.

Joseph was looking at her with old, tired eyes as he said," What happened to your husband and your furniture?" he whispered so that he wouldn't wake her daughter." I beg your pardon." Nicole snapped! "I am sorry if I am being rude, " he answered, but I can't imagine you being in this big house with your handicapped daughter and not having a husband." "I do" she said in a soft voice, "He passed away" "Oh, I am so sorry" Joseph said, Nicole said, "It's ok, It's been about a year, he was on a business trip in Maryland and as he was walking across the street, He was struck by a car and died instantly, the man that hit him swerved to avoid him and hit a tree and he also Died, that is what I heard. 'That is so sad', Joseph said, "do you know who the other man was? 'No,' Nicole said; I heard his body was sent back to

New Jersey, where he was from, and I never found out. I live everyday wondering who he was, and to make matters worse, we are in debt for 60,000, my husband got a loan for the car he bought me for my birthday and He financed new furniture and to pay for medical bills for Sam. That is why I don't have a car or furniture anymore. They repossessed it all. I only have enough money to live for now. Oh! Forgive me for going on like this "No, It's quite alright" Joseph said, If you don't Mind me asking, What is the disease that Sammy has? Nicole looked at him with tears in her eyes and told him the whole story. They spoke for hours, and by the time it was light outside, she knew she had grown to like Joseph.

As the morning approached, Nicole walked over and tucked Sam in her sleeping bag since they were not going anywhere for a while, it seemed she might as well let her sleep. Then she went over and sat with her new guest and had a cup of tea. During their conversation Joseph asked," Is there any way that Sammy can be helped"? He asked in a stuttering, hesitant way. "Yes there is a way, Nicole said, but she needs a special surgery to replace the bones with titanium rods to help her stand without crutches, but it costs like 100 thousand dollars. Joseph looked at her with pity and apologized. "Why are you sorry? she asked. Joseph answered," because at one time in my life I was a very rich man, but spiritually poor, and here you are rich in faith and struggling to survive","I am ashamed of myself" he said as he lowered his head into his hands. Nicole saw the pain in the man's eyes and knew that he was sincere. 'It's ok, she said. God will help us find a way, I know He will, I have enough faith for both of us. They ended the conversation, then Nicole went over to Sammy sleeping on the floor and slipped beside her in the xlarge sleeping bag and left the other one for her guest, in case he wanted to lay down. Hours went by; it was now about noon time, and still no sign of help.

As the day went on, Sammy and Joseph kept busy playing Monopoly on the floor in front of the make-believe fireplace they made with old gift boxes and wrapping paper that they found in the closet. Nicole looked at the calendar in the kitchen and noticed that it was exactly one month until Christmas. They had been snowed in for a week now with no phone or furniture, and they were running low on food, but she made a new friend, and so did her daughter, as if God sent him to keep us company during the storm. That made her think to herself, Let me pray for God to help us, to send us help for Joseph and herself and her daughter.

Nicole made an arm sling out of one of her scarves and put Joseph's arm in it while it healed. She Made Chicken for dinner that she had in her freezer. She looked in the refrigerator and saw that they were running very low on everything, so she decided to just make half portions for them all to save whatever food she had left until, God willing, they were rescued. Because she lived on a cult de sac, there were no other houses close to her, and the neighbors up the street were away on business in another country. That made her think, Why was Joseph driving here in the night in this deserted area? Where was he going? Since they were friends now, she decided to ask him. "Excuse me, Joseph she said." Looking up from the board game he was playing with her daughter, he said, "Yes? She asked," Where were you going the night you crashed into the tree? I'm just curious because no one comes down this street, and there are no other houses here?" "I was wondering about that since I saw the accident." He looked at her like he saw a ghost and said, "To be honest, I really don't remember." I guess I hit my head so hard that I don't even remember why I was here in Hope, Pennsylvania, in the first place." Nicole thought that it was strange that he didn't remember why he came here, but she figured that the head injury might be worse than she had expected, so she dropped the conversation and went back to the kitchen to finish dinner.

Another whole day went by, and Nicole kept wondering if they would ever be rescued. After changing Joseph's bandages once again, she heard a loud band outside. Sammy lifted her Frail body and said," See Joseph, we are going to be rescued and they will fix your arm and cuts, and you will be ok again". Joseph looked at her with happiness in his eyes and said, "Thank you, I hope so." Nicole could not believe how much compassion her daughter had shown to this man that we have had as a guest for a week now. She was an introverted child and didn't have many friends. It was a blessing. This man changed her completely.

Nicole ran to the front door, but it didn't open, in fear that she would be covered in a pile of snow, she waited a few minutes, then yelled "We are in here." The truck fell silent; Nicole's heart dropped. Did they leave? She whispered. Then there was a loud bang and the front door flew open and four men and a paramedic stood there In Front of her. "My God! one man said, "How long have you people been here?" Nicole said" about a week". "This man was involved in a car accident and needed medical attention." " I know, the paramedic said, we heard of an accident, but we couldn't get to you because the roads were too bad. "How much snow did we get?" she asked in surprise, "the man said about 4 feet, total the biggest storm we have ever gotten in these parts." Nicole said, "This man, his name is Joseph. He has a broken arm; I made a sling and helped heal his wounds. The medic walked over to Joseph and said "Hello sir, are you ok?" Can you walk"? Joseph with a smile on his face said, " Yes, I think so." As the 4 men helped Joseph to the front door, He stopped and gave Nicole a big hug and whispered in her eye" "I don't know how I will ever repay you for what you have done for me" She whispered back," You already have". He turned around and saw Sammy standing there with tears running down her cheeks, "I'll miss you, Joseph, " she said. He said back, "I'll miss you too, but we will see each other again, one day, I am sure of it." Take care of your mom She said, I will, then he was gone.

Three weeks had passed since that day, The snow was almost completely gone. With a hundred dollars in her pocket that her daughter gave to her from her piggy bank, Nicole walked 3 long miles to the store to get some food. As she was walking, she kept thinking about Joseph and I was wondering how he was doing. She decided to stop and check the mail on her way back She looked through the mail and saw Sammy watching her from the window, she waved and looked at the electric bill, water bill and a letter from an unknown address. She didn't recognize the handwriting, but she opened it anyway. It was from a law firm, Meyer and Johnson. She was getting nervous. What else do they want from me? she thought to herself, so she started to read the letter it said;

Mrs. Cimino,

My name is John Meyer. I need to see you in my office at nine am on December 24th.

I will send a car to come and get your daughter. I will explain everything then. Thank you

Signed,
John Meyer, esq.

The address and the office were located in Baltimore, Maryland, the same place where her husband was killed. Who was this? and what did they want? Today was the 23rd of December, she thought to herself, Should I go? Who is this lawyer? These thoughts kept going through her head She went inside and told her daughter, she didn't get the response she thought she would get instead, Sammy yelled, "Let's go"? So Nicole agreed, I need to see what this is about and they are picking us up, so that's good, because Baltimore was 3 hours away from where she lived so she put away the food she bought at the store and curled up on the floor with Sammy and went to sleep for the night, Thanking God for what they have each and every day.

The next morning, It was Christmas eve, at Nicole and Sammy woke up early, made breakfast and got dressed, Nicole was a little nervous about this trip, What was this really about? but decided to go anyway. At exactly 9 am, a limo pulled up in front of the house. The driver got out and walked around to the passenger's side and opened the door, Nicole and Sam just stood there in shock, "A limo"? She asked the driver, as she helped Sammy walk to the car, "Yes, the driver said," My name is Darryl, Are you ready for your trip"? Sammy yelled, " Yes", Nicole didn't share the same sentiment as her daughter. she asked Darryl, " Where are we going?" He replied," You will find out soon enough." That response made Nicole feel kind of uneasy, but what did she have to lose? She had lost it all already, so they got into the car and were on their way to an unknown destination.

Three hours later they pulled up in front of a huge building, with the names Meyer and Johnson law firm on the outside. Darryl got out and walked around to the other side, where Nicole and her daughter sat patiently. He opened the door and said," Follow me," He even took Sammy's hand to help her walk. They followed him into the building, went into an elevator and up to the 23rd floor. When they reached the floor , he led them into a conference room and told them to wait there for someone to be with them shortly. Nicole noticed that there were two bottles of water and 2 sandwiches and chips on the table in front of them, and before Darryl walked out, he said" please eat" that is your lunch? "Lunch"? Nicole asked, "What kind of law firm offers lunch to people they don't know". "What is going on"? He just smiled and walked out.

"Where are we"? Sammy asked her mother. "I'm not sure, honey," was her reply. Just as she spoke, the door opened and a man about 40 years of age with black hair and glasses stood before them." Nicole Cimino", I am miles Johnson, he said extending a hand she stood to shake his hand and he said" Please sit" and pointed to the chair behind her. "Hello Samantha", He said, "how was the ride". "It was long, but good", she replied.

Nicole looked the man in the eyes and said" Please tell me why you had a limo driver pick up myself and my handicapped daughter and drive for 3 hours, I know it wasn't to give us a sandwich and a drink? " Of course not", he said. Will get to that in a minute.

"Let me get my paperwork, " looking through a file on the desk in front of him, He said "ok I got it,

"Are you the wife of John Cimino? "

" Yes, " she said, "but how do you know John?"

"I know that he died in a car accident," he said

In shock, she replied, " How do you know that"?

Nicole could not believe what she was hearing. Mr. Johnson handed her an envelope. She slowly took it from him. She noticed it had her name on it. "What's this" She asked "Open it", He said, "it's for you". Nicole carefully opened the envelope and took out the document that was inside, when she looked at it, she couldn't speak. It was a check for 5 million dollars. "How"? "Why, "Who? She couldn't get the words out. "Let me explain," Mr. Johnson said, When your husband was killed, the driver that hit him felt unbelievably bad, as he lay there in the hospital on his deathbed, he decided to sign over all of his assets to the man's wife and daughter. That is you, Mrs. Cimino. " That's impossible",

Nicole said. I heard the man crashed into a tree after he hit my husband only to die himself. " That is true, " Johnson said, but after lying in a coma for 5 days, after he came to, he knew he didn't have long to live because he found a brain tumor that he didn't know he had and if it wasn't for the accident he would have never known. So he called me. I am his attorney. He asked me to find out if the man he killed had a family. When I found you, he told me to leave it all to you and your daughter, because he was so sorry. He was a wealthy, rude businessman and when he was in the coma, he said it changed his life, so that is why he did what he did, before he died. Nicole looked stunned, then she asked What was the man's name"? Mr. Johnson replied, " Joseph Thomas". Nicole dropped the envelope and collapsed on the floor.

When Nicole came to, her daughter was standing over her with a big smile on her face and said," See, I told you, Mommy, Joseph is our guardian angel". Mr. Johnson helped Nicole off the floor, but she just stood there in disbelief. " No she said, He could not have left this to me in his will, he was just at my house for a week, he was in an accident and I saved him, also he said he was broke and didn't have any money left, how could this be?" "Mrs. Cimino, Mr. Johnson with a bewildered look on his face said, " Joseph Thomas has been dead for over a year, I am sorry to tell you that but that was not the same man. "Oh my God, Nicole shouted, "Maybe he is an angel." Miles just looked at her strangely and handed her another envelope, here this was also left for you, it is for your eyes only, nobody else is allowed to read it. She took the envelope and said" what else can it be? he already left me every-thing? "She took the envelope from him, not knowing what to find in it this time, walking over to the window so she can be by herself she opened it and found herself staring at a blank piece of paper, it said on the top, "hold up to the sun to read, invisible ink" She did as it in-structed and held it up towards the sunlight shining through the big window, and as she did that, the working came into view the letter said:

Dear Nicole,

Thank you for caring for me during the accident and that horrible snowstorm; when you had nothing for yourself to live, you did everything to save my life. That shows the kind of person that you are. I waited to give you this gift because I wanted to see if you really needed it; while I was in a coma, I was approached by an angel of God and he told me that I was going to be sent back to earth to make amends for how I left my life, my body will be in the coma but my spirit will be where he sent me, that is all I remember, then I was looking at you from my car that was embedded in a tree, but I did not remember my life before the accident, when I came out of the coma I remembered everything and I knew what I had to do to repay you, before I left this earth. I am so happy that I got the chance to spend time with you and your daughter and that I got a second chance to do good with my money before I left this earth, and I thank God for giving me a second chance. Please take the money and get Sammy her surgery, reclaim your belongings, pay off your bills and live a happy life. I will be watching over you always. And please make sure to go back to church and thank God for everything he has done for you and for me. This letter is for your eyes only, It will disappear after it is read.

p.s. Your husband sends his love.

God bless,
your guardian Angel
Joseph

Nicole started crying, and as the tears rolled down her face to the letter, the wording started to disappear again until she was staring at a blank piece of paper in her hand once again. With tears in her eyes, Nicole said, " Thank you, Mr. Johnson, for finding me, but why did you wait this long?" "Because he said, the instructions were very clear, it said to not give you the envelope until Christmas Eve. He wanted you to have the best Christmas ever with your daughter. Can I ask?

Johnson said, "Why did he give you a blank piece of paper?" that's odd."

She quickly answered, "I am not sure, and I will never find out either, as she winked at Sammy, who was watching her from a distance with a smile on her face.

Months went by, Nicole was standing at her front door yelling to the furniture men "Please put the couch and TV next to the fireplace. " The moving men looked at each other strangely and said" What fireplace? Nicole pointed to a place in the corner; all they saw was a bunch of rolled-up wrapping paper and a few boxes taped together that seemed to form what they guessed was a fireplace. They didn't agree with her, they just carried the furniture in and sat it next to her paper fireplace, then went on their way. As Nicole was getting ready to pick up Sammy from school, She got into the driver's seat of her brand-new Ford Expedition. She decided to check the mail first. She opened the mailbox and took out a few letters, one was a letter that she sent to Meyer and Johnson law firm thanking her for everything, she noticed it was returned and said address unknown. "What?" How can this be? Let me call them and find out. Did they go out of business or move to another location? She grabbed her cell phone and dialed the number she said for the company, it rang for a while, then a lady answered, hello, St. Joseph Catholic church office, can I help you? Nicole stuttered, but got the words out? "Hello this is Nicole Cimino, isn't this the law office of Meyer and Johnson "? No Mame, The lady said, This is St. Joseph Catholic church. Nicole replied, how long have you had this number? The lady said, "about 20 years why"? Nicole bewildered asked, "Are you still located in Baltimore Maryland?" "Baltimore? the lady exclaimed, "that's a long way off, we are located in a small town in Pennsylvania called, Hope"

Nicole dropped the phone to the ground, looked up and said, "That was you, God, wasn't it"?

"you wanted me to go back to church, so you are leading me to a church called St. Joseph" hello? Hello? Mame, are you there? the voice yelled at the other end of the line. Nicole snapped out of the trance and picked up the phone," yes I am sorry, it's just that I live in Hope ,Pa and I never saw or heard of a church called St. Joseph here, where are you located?" "Well said the women, "we are located right at the end of the Grammar school road , Nicole answered," but, we only have one school in Hope, I never saw a church here, I know of St. John's in the next town over but not here." "The voice on the other end of the line said ,"were you looking for one?"

Nicole thought for a minute and said, "I guess I wasn't. So what are your mass times?

The lady told her the mass times and where to find the church, so Nicole hung up the phone and

drove to pick up her daughter from school. Thank God after Sammy got her surgery she was able to walk again without crutches. as Nicole pulled into the school parking lot, she decided to drive around the block to look for this church and she didn't find it. but as she was turning around to leave, she saw a bright light in her rearview mirror. She stopped the car, put it in park and got out. What she saw in front of her was the biggest, most beautiful church steeple that she had ever seen. It was so brightly lit and Under it was the writing, St. Joseph Catholic church. Why hadn't she noticed it before? She walked up to the church doors and it said, welcome back, we missed you. She turned around, but no one was around. Was this a sign? Is this place real or just a figment of my imagination, she thought to herself. As she was daydreaming, she heard a voice from behind her, " are you looking to go to mass?", Nicole quickly turned around and saw a priest standing there, where did he come from? She thought. Oh, yes, she said, " I am thinking about coming back to church"? "Are you Catholic," the priest said ." yes, I am, she said, but I have not been to church in awhile; I am Nicole Cimino, she said, extending her hand towards the priest

"I need to come back". He reached and shook her hand. Then she said, I used to work at my church's office years ago, but I had to stop working because of my handicapped daughter, but now I can work a part-time job again. "Well he said, I am Father O'Malley and we have an opening in the office for a part time receptionist if you are interested. Nicole couldn't believe what she was hearing, everything she ever dreamed of was happening in her life all due to a man named Joseph that she met on a snowy winter day. She was just curious and asked Father, "How long has this Parish been here?" I have lived in Hope for 20 years and never noticed it before. His response was the same as the receptionist's that she spoke to that morning when she called the office, he said," Were you looking?". "I guess not," She said. Then thought to herself, "Was I really that out of it that I did not notice a big steeple behind my daughter's school?" I guess I will never know. Looking up at the sky, she smiled.

Then she shook Father's hand and told him she would be in the office the next morning to apply

and to join the Parish. Then she went to pick up Sammy and told her the story on the way home. She still wasn't too sure as she was telling the story if it really happened, but when she told her daughter, Sammy didn't seem too shocked to hear that the law firm that they both went to in Maryland was now a Catholic church, named St. Joseph's in their home town of Hope, Pa. Although Nicole still wasn't sure how that happened, she just called it divine intervention.

As they were driving away, Nicole looked in her rearview mirror to make sure that the church steeple was still there and that it wasn't all in her imagination, but she smiled to see that it was there, and it was shining brighter than ever. She drove away towards a new life and a new outlook on the future. She knows they will never be alone because God will be watching over them, and she will always be thankful that he sent her a man named Joseph Thomas that changed her life.

Join Nicole Cimino and her handicapped daughter on their adventure when they are trapped in their home at Christmas time during the storm of the century waiting for someone to rescue them, but there is a light at the end of the tunnel.